The Curse of the Sapphire Skull

Maverick

Chapter Readers

'The Curse of the Sapphire Skull'
An original concept by Elizabeth Dale
© Elizabeth Dale 2022

Illustrated by Hannah McCaffery

Published by MAVERICK ARTS PUBLISHING LTD
Studio 11, City Business Centre, 6 Brighton Road,
Horsham, West Sussex, RH13 5BB
© Maverick Arts Publishing Limited August 2022
+44 (0)1403 256941

A CIP catalogue record for this book is available at the British Library.

ISBN 978-1-84886-919-6

www.maverickbooks.co.uk

This book is rated as: Grey Band (Guided Reading)

The Curse of the Sapphire Skull

Written by Elizabeth Dale

Illustrated by
Hannah McCaffery

Chapter 1

It was a glorious, sunny morning. The strong wind was whipping up the most amazing waves as Zac and his grandad hurried down the cliff. Zac smiled happily. It was so early, they had the beautiful, sandy beach all to themselves—just how they loved it!

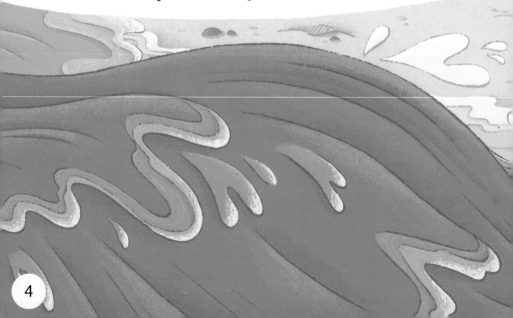

Zac gasped at the cold as he ran into the sea. His grandad followed but Zac went even deeper. Soon he was nearly up to his knees. "Come in more, Grandad!" he cried. "It's fun!"

His grandad chuckled. "Oooh, it's so cold..." he said as he gingerly waded further in. Suddenly, a huge wave came thundering in and **SPLASH!**

"Oh!"

They both shrieked in shock as the water hit them.

Zac's shorts and Grandad's trousers were totally soaked! They laughed at the sight of each other but, whilst Grandad quickly waded out of the sea, Zac continued splashing through the waves. After all, he couldn't really get much wetter!

Zac was about to turn and start running back to his grandad when he noticed something round and gold rolling backwards and forwards in the surf. The closer he got to it, the more amazing it looked. But only when he picked it up, did he realise what it was. A skull! A gold skull with an eerie, smiling mouth and dazzling blue eyes!

Zac couldn't believe what he saw. It was larger than a human skull and totally amazing! He shook the water out of it and turned it over in his hands. The wet gold glinted in the sunlight, and the blue eyes stared back at him. He just *had* to show this to Grandad!

"Look, Grandad, look!" he cried, racing back to him, holding out the skull. "Look what I found!"

Grandad looked up from unrolling his wet trousers and just stood there, staring at it in wonder. "What a clever boy!" he cried. "What an incredible find! It seems to be moulded in real gold."

"Isn't it brilliant?" cried Zac, giving it to him. "Oh, those blue glass eyes are so cool!"

His grandad shook his head. "I think they might be large sapphires rather than glass," he said. "They're really precious stones!"

"Wow!" said Zac. "And it's here on our beach. How amazing! I wonder how it got here? Maybe robbers hid it in the caves? And the sea washed it out? Do you think it was stolen from a jewellers?"

"I don't think so," said Grandad. "It looks very old to me. Come on, let's take it home and see what we can find out about it."

"Okay," said Zac, trying to hide his disappointment. For a moment, he'd imagined that a whole heap of reward money—just perfect for buying a bike—might be coming his way. "So, it's not that valuable then?" he asked, just to be sure.

His grandad tore his eyes away from the skull and smiled at Zac. "On the contrary," he said, "it could just be very valuable indeed."

Chapter 2

Zac wrapped the skull in his jumper to protect it and proudly carried it up the cliff and back to the house his family shared with Grandad. His mum greeted them at the door.

"Oh my goodness! You're soaking wet!" she cried.

Zac had totally forgotten about that. "It's fine," he said. "Look what I found on the beach, Mum!" And he carefully unwrapped the skull.

"Isn't it beautiful, Caz?" said Grandad.

"Amazing!" she gasped.

"I think it could be an ancient artefact," said Grandad. "We're going up to my room to do some research, aren't we, Zac?"

"Yep!" he nodded happily.

"But what about breakfast?" asked his mum. "You rushed out early. I was going to make pancakes."

Zac hesitated.

"Could we eat them upstairs?" Grandad asked.

Mum laughed. "Okay, I'll bring you two each!"

Zac grinned. "Brilliant! But make mine four, please!"

They raced up to Grandad's room. Zac was forever amazed at how many things Grandad had crammed in there. He used to be an archaeologist, travelling the world going from dig to dig, finding ancient pottery, jewels, weapons and coins. There were shelves and shelves of old books with Grandad's favourite finds laid out in front. And, in one corner, a tiny statue of a Greek god stared

up, spear raised, as though about to attack.

"Right!" said Grandad, sitting in his chair at his old, oak desk. "Give the skull to me, lad. Let me have a proper look!" And he picked up his magnifying glass and inspected the whole skull closely. He smiled as he ran his fingers over the gold teeth.

"Exquisite!" he said. "You've made a great find here, Zac. It reminds me of something... I think it might possibly be Ancient Greek." He carefully placed the skull on a shelf, and switched on his computer. Then he browsed the titles of his old books on the bookshelves.

"What can I do? I want to help," said Zac.

"Of course you do," said Grandad. "You're a whizz on computers. Why don't you search 'Ancient Greek gold skulls' while I look in this brilliant book!" And he held up a huge book titled 'Ancient Greek Treasures.'

"Okay!" Zac smiled. Searching the web was fun. 'Ancient Greek skulls' didn't produce anything like their one, neither did 'blue-eyed gold skulls' but when he tried 'Ancient Greek gold skulls with sapphire eyes', he found a website with a drawing that looked just like their skull.

"Got it!" he cried triumphantly. "I'm sure this is it! Look, it's called 'The Sapphire Skull' because of its blue eyes. They really are sapphires, Grandad! See!"

Grandad peered over his shoulder. "You're right!" he cried. "That's just like our skull! Well done, Zac!"

There wasn't much about it online—simply that it had been lost centuries before—but now that Grandad knew its name, he could look it up in the index and soon found it in his book.

"My goodness, can you believe it... it's cursed!" he cried, turning to Zac, his eyes shining. "Listen!" He read: "The Sapphire Skull was famous for its evil curse. In an instant, it could turn its victims' words into pure gibberish and few of those afflicted could ever reverse the curse. The skull was being transported from Crete to Athens one stormy night, when the captain and first mate started talking nonsense. The crew didn't understand their shouting until it was too late: they failed to steer past some jagged rocks and the ship struck them and sank.

Only a cabin boy managed to swim to shore. The rest of the crew and the Sapphire Skull were lost forever!"

Zac listened, open-mouthed. "Not forever," he said, gazing at the Sapphire Skull. "We found it, washed up from the wreck onto our beach. We have got the famous cursed skull!"

Chapter 3

Zac was dancing around the room when his mum came in with pancakes covered with strawberries and cream.

"What's going on?!" she asked, laughing.

"We have only got a genuine Ancient Greek Sapphire Skull—that's actually cursed!" cried Zac.

"Hold on a minute," smiled Grandad. "We know there was a cursed skull just like this. But we don't know that we have the real one. This might be a copy."

Zac's face fell. "A copy?!" he said. "Just a copy?"

"It could be," said Grandad. "Someone might have made it as a prop for a play or for an exhibition. We can't be sure we have the real Sapphire Skull. But we'll get it checked at the museum today. Louise there has the perfect equipment to date things. Plus, she has lots of historical manuscripts I used to study when I worked there. Hopefully they can tell us far more about the real Sapphire Skull and its curse. I can't wait to discover all about it."

"Or if we have the real one! Hurry, Grandad, eat your pancakes," said Zac, starting on his plateful—and wishing he hadn't actually asked for four!

Grandad laughed. "Thank you, Caz," he said, taking his plate from her. "They look far too delicious to be rushed, I'm going to savour every single mouthful."

"Great, enjoy!" she said. "I'm going shopping with my friend, Sarah, now. Have fun, you two. I hope it is the real skull."

Zac gobbled down his pancakes at record speed but, by the time he'd eaten all four, Grandad was still on his second. He was so slow! But finally, he finished too.

"At last!" said Zac, waving his arms in celebration.

"Now we can... **NO!**"

His waving arm accidentally knocked the skull and it started to wobble precariously on the edge of the shelf.

"I've got it!" cried Grandad, reaching up to steady it. But somehow, in his haste, he knocked the skull more and it started to fall right off. "Whoops!" he muttered, scrabbling to catch it. Zac stared in horror as the skull slipped right through Grandad's fingers and landed on the floor with a crash.

"Ho raed!" Grandad cried.

Zac, in the middle of picking up the skull, turned. *What?!*

Grandad stared back in horror. He grabbed Zac's arm. "Ho on, Caz!" he said. "On Caz! On!"

Zac gazed at Grandad blankly. What was he saying? Why did he keep calling him Caz? That was his mum's name. Was he hallucinating? Did he think Zac was his mum? Or had he suddenly gone blind? But then Grandad picked up his book. So he *could* see.

Zac forced a laugh. His grandad had the weirdest sense of humour. "Come on, stop messing around, Grandad," he said. "We need to get to the museum quick."

"Sey, Caz!" cried Grandad. "Ew od!"

Zac frowned. *He* wasn't the one being odd.

"Kool!" Grandad said.

Zac didn't think what was happening was cool. His grandad jabbed the page hard. "Kool!" he repeated.

And then the terrible truth hit Zac. His grandad was pointing to the line in his book that mentioned the curse of the Sapphire Skull. And he was talking gibberish.

"No!" he cried. "Oh no! No! Grandad! You're cursed?"

His grandad nodded sadly.

"Oh, Grandad, I'm so sorry! This is terrible!" Zac cried, hugging him. "Don't worry," he added, trying to sound cheerful. "We'll sort this, Grandad. People managed to break the curse in the past, we'll do it too. We can get you back to normal. We can!"

"Sey, ew nac," said Grandad.

Zac frowned. "Ew nac," he repeated. "Look, all we have to do is find out how you annoyed the skull. It must be something only you did. Otherwise why wouldn't it curse me too? Maybe if we can reverse what you did, the skull will be happy again?"

Grandad smiled, nodding, and Zac grinned back. But he was churning inside. He didn't know if he could do this. With his grandad talking gibberish and unable to explain what to do or how they might break the curse, he felt as though it was up to him alone to work out how to do it. When he'd said he couldn't wait to find out if the skull was real, he really, really hadn't wanted to find out this way!

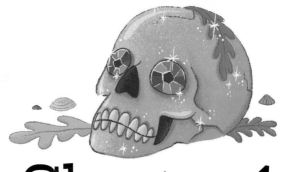

Chapter 4

Grandad started reading out loud from his book, but it was total gibberish, so Zac took over.

"No one knew why the curse was inflicted on anyone," he read. "And only a few managed to reverse it."

Zac paused and flicked ahead through the book and frowned. "But it doesn't say anywhere how they broke the curse!" he cried. "It's so frustrating! What should we do, Grandad?"

"Og dna ees Esiuol," Grandad replied, which wasn't any use. Zac went back to the internet. There could be more up-to-date info there. Whilst scrolling through sites, he also rang his mum. He needed someone to talk to.

Someone who made sense when they talked back! "Answer, Mum, please!" he begged as her mobile rang, but she didn't. Nothing was going his way.

"Ew evah ot og ot Esiuol!" his grandad cried again. "Ehs nac pleh su!"

Zac looked at his grandad miserably. His gibberish was making his head ache. And then, finally, he found 'Sapphire Skull' on another site, with more information.

"Grandad!" he cried. "It says here that the curse has to be reversed within 6 days! No! Otherwise..." he stopped. The words that followed were impossible to read out to Grandad: '*Otherwise the victim was afflicted for life*'. It was impossible even to think about. Only 6 days to break it... That was nowhere near long enough!

"Oh, what are we going to do?!" he wailed.

Grandad thrust a piece of paper at Zac. He'd scribbled a message:

EW EVAH OT OG DNA EES ESIUOL TA EHT MUESUM! EHS LLIW PLEH SU!

Zac gazed at it in despair. He was even more confused than ever! What had DNA got to do with it? Did Grandad have to do a DNA test? Why? It didn't make sense.

Zac looked up. His grandad was gazing at him hopefully, expecting that Zac would somehow understand. It was impossible—he needed help! Desperately he rang his mum again, while trying to make sense of the words. Still no answer. "Oh, who can help me?!" he cried.

Grandad was adding to his note. **ESIUOL!** he scribbled.

And then it came to Zac. There *was* someone who might just be able to help them. "Louise at the museum!" he cried.

"Yarooh!" cried his grandad, jabbing his finger at his note. And suddenly Zac saw it. Grandad had written LOUISE backwards! He looked at the words above it, in the rest of the note. They were backwards too! "We have to go and see Louise at the museum!" he deciphered. "She will help us!"

"Sey!" cried Grandad. "Yarooh!"

"Yes!" Zac translated. "Hooray! Oh, hooray indeed, Grandad!" Zac jumped up and hugged him. He was so pleased, he could have cried. Grandad wasn't speaking total nonsense, he was simply talking backwards! Now he could understand what Grandad was saying, he wasn't alone! They could break the curse together!

Chapter 5

As they prepared to go to the museum, Zac picked up the skull.

"On!" cried Grandad.

"No? Why not?" asked Zac. "Oh, I guess we don't need to take it now, do we? We know it's the real Sapphire Skull."

"Sey," Grandad replied. And then he wrote:

DNA EW T'NOD TNAW OT KSIR GNIGAMAD RO GNISOL TI!

"Oh, you're right!" said Zac, who was getting quicker at deciphering Grandad's words. "We need to keep it really safe so we can reverse your curse."

Grandad was writing again. Zac read, 'Plus, we don't want it to accidentally curse someone else on the way!' He smiled. "Wow! Good thinking, Grandad! After all, we don't know what brings on the curse."

Zac rang the museum and quickly told Louise about the Sapphire Skull and the curse on Grandad.

"Oh my goodness!" she cried. "How absolutely terrible!"

"I know," said Zac. "Some people in Ancient Greece managed to reverse the curse, but we don't know how. Grandad thought there might possibly be an explanation in one of the Ancient Greek manuscripts at the museum. We'd like to come and look at them, please."

"Of course!" she said. "I'll get them out ready for you."

Because Zac's mum had taken the car, they had to catch the bus to the museum. Their neighbour, Olive, was already at the bus stop. She smiled at them and, before Zac could stop him, Grandad said, "Olleh, evilo!"

Olive's smile turned to a frown. "Evil O!" she cried. "How rude!"

"Ho... ho..." Grandad began, going red.

"And now you're laughing at me!" she spluttered.

"No he isn't!" Zac cried, quickly. "I'm sorry, Grandad's not very well, he's, er, got a bad throat, he can't speak very clearly."

Olive's eyes narrowed in suspicion. "I think I heard him clearly enough."

Zac gulped. "Really, Olive, he's just poorly. He just needs to see the..."

"Pots!" cried Grandad, sticking out his arm.

Olive stared blankly. "See the pots?"

"No, look!" cried Zac, waving wildly as a bus approached fast. "Stop!"

Fortunately, it did. "Don't say a word to anyone!" Zac whispered to Grandad as they waited to get on behind Olive. "I'll pay the fare."

Grandad was doing well. He managed to stay silent all the journey until a man across the aisle asked him the time and he replied, "Sey, net ot owt."

"Why do I have to say that rubbish?" asked the man crossly, and Zac had to quickly interrupt and tell him it was ten to two.

Fortunately, they got to the museum without further incident and were soon safely inside Louise's office. She had a huge pile of folders on her desk.

"I'm really sorry to hear what's happened," she said. "Hopefully these documents might be useful. But some of them are in Ancient Greek and it's such a difficult language. Here's our dictionary. I'm afraid I'll have to leave you to it. I've got an important meeting starting right now but I'll come back as soon as I can!"

"Knaht uoy," said Grandad and they both set to work, Zac just looking at documents written in English. Eventually, he found one about the skull, with drawings of people lying down in front of it.

"Look! Did the skull send them to sleep?" Zac asked Grandad, showing him.

Grandad explained that he thought that they were prostrating themselves by way of apology, to get the skull to reverse the curse. He showed Zac a really useful document he'd just found, which was actually describing how to reverse the curse, but he was having difficulty translating it. He really needed his own Ancient Greek dictionary at home, which was much bigger and filled with notes he'd made over the years to help him with translations.

"Well, let's go home then!" said Zac. "You take photos of the pages you need and I'll leave Louise a message, telling her what we've done."

As he quickly wrote the note, Zac was already worrying about their journey home and who Grandad might upset! "I'll order us a taxi," he said, "it'll be easier than catching the bus."

But it wasn't. The young taxi driver was very chatty, and he kept asking Grandad questions, which Zac jumped in quick to answer.

"What's the matter with the old man?" the driver asked Zac. "Is he alright?"

"What?"

"Has he, you know, lost his marbles?"

That was too much for Grandad. "Selbram! I evah ton tsol ym selbram!" he yelled in frustration.

The driver braked and pulled over. "What on earth is he going on about?! I think you'd best get out. I can't drive with him yelling like that!"

"No, you've got it wrong," said Zac. "He just doesn't speak English, he speaks... er... er... Esperanto! Please just drive us home. He won't say anything again, will you, Grandad?"

Grandad shook his head. Not if he could help it!

Chapter 6

Fortunately, the taxi driver stopped talking to them after that. As soon as they got back, Zac and Grandad rushed up to his room. Zac's mum wasn't back so at least they didn't need to worry her yet, they just had to get on with reversing the curse.

"Why don't you just try prostrating yourself, like the people did in those drawings, and simply say sorry," proposed Zac.

So Grandad tried. "Yrros!" he said.

"Maybe you have to say it the right way round?" Zac suggested.

Grandad frowned. "I t'nac!"

"Yes you can!" said Zac and he wrote 'YRROS' on a piece of paper.

"Sorry!" said Grandad, reading it out loud backwards. But then he said, "Did ti krow?"

Oh no! He hadn't broken the curse.

So Grandad got up, explaining to Zac that he'd continue translating the ancient document from the museum to try to find out how others broke the curse. At least that's what Zac guessed he said. Grandad didn't have time to write it down.

As there was little Zac could do while Grandad was busy translating, he made him a much-needed coffee.

"How are you getting on?" Zac asked eagerly, when he returned.

"Yako," said Grandad. He explained that the skull put the curse on anyone who disrespected it.

"But you didn't..." Zac began. And then he remembered. "Of course! You dropped it. If that isn't disrespectful, I don't know what is!"

Grandad nodded, still focusing on his translation. Suddenly he gasped and looked up at Zac in horror.

"What?" asked Zac. "What's wrong?"

Grandad scribbled fast and Zac leant across, deciphering Grandad's words as he wrote them.

"The website translated the ancient documents wrongly," he said, slowly. "We don't have 6 days to reverse the curse." Zac gasped. "No! How long do we have? 5 days? 4 days? 3?"

Grandad kept shaking his head. And then he wrote the terrible words: '6 sruoh!'

"6 hours!" Zac cried, appalled. "No! But you were cursed... when... around 11 this morning? So we've only got until 5 to reverse it!"

He looked at his watch. It was half-past 4. They had just half an hour to reverse the curse! No wonder Grandad looked so upset.

Inside, Zac was panicking like mad, but he forced a smile. He had to appear calm for Grandad's sake.

"That's okay," he said. "We've got a whole thirty minutes. We can do this. Your brilliant dictionary is helping you understand everything. We just need to know what you have to say when you prostrate yourself—and then do it."

Zac's brain whirred as his grandad carried on translating. This was all his fault. If he hadn't knocked the skull, Grandad wouldn't have tried to steady it and knocked it onto the floor. If Grandad was stuck talking backwards for the rest of his life, he'd never forgive himself. Never!

"Tog ti!" Grandad cried.

He excitedly scribbled a note explaining that his disrespect had really annoyed the skull. All he had to do was show he was sorry and tell it a joke it had never heard before to make it happy again!

"A joke!" Zac cried. "Is that all? It's from Ancient Greece. There must be loads of modern jokes it doesn't know. Like... um..." But his mind went totally blank. He couldn't think of a single one! Neither could Grandad.

Desperately, Zac turned to the internet. "Here's one!" he cried, pointing to the screen.

Grandad read it, smiled and lay down.

"Hold on, I've got to write it backwards for you, so you read it forwards for the skull to understand!" Zac said. He did so quickly and passed it to Grandad, still lying on the floor. In a loud, clear voice he read, "Do you think I can jump higher than this house? Of course I can—this house can't jump!"

Zac grinned and said, "Hooray!"

And Grandad smiled—and said, "Yarooh!"

Zac groaned. The curse still hadn't been broken. What had they done wrong? Was Grandad's document—or his translation—inaccurate? Or was the joke so awful that the skull didn't find it funny? Maybe it didn't understand it?

Suddenly, it hit Zac. Of course! That was it! "The skull's from Ancient Greece!" he cried. "That's the only language it knows! It doesn't understand English so it didn't understand our joke! You need to translate it into Ancient Greek, Grandad!"

"Sey!" cried Grandad.

He worked away, translating it, while Zac watched the clock, worrying. It was nearly five to 5. They didn't know the exact time the curse had been put on Grandad. What if it had been five to 11? Or ten to? They only had 6 hours to break it! The deadline could have passed already!

Finally, Grandad triumphantly showed Zac what he'd written. But it was lines of strange Greek letters.

"Oh Grandad!" Zac cried. "These letters are all so weird!

I have to write the words backwards for you to read them right. But it'll take me ages. We don't have time!"

Grandad's frown turned to a smile. "I wonk!" he cried, snatching his mirror from the wall. He lay down in front of the skull, tipped the mirror so he could see the words reflected in reverse and spoke them forwards—correctly!

It was the worst gibberish Zac had ever heard, but he hoped that was simply because it was Ancient Greek. Would the skull understand? Would it like the joke? Could it possibly work?

Chapter 7

There was silence. Grandad didn't dare speak. What if it hadn't worked?

Suddenly, there was a deep roaring sound. It was coming from the skull—and it sounded *really* annoyed.

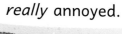

Zac stared at Grandad in horror. A tingle of fear went down his spine. Did the skull not like  their joke? Was he about to be cursed too? And then the roar grew louder and developed—into laughter! The skull was laughing at their joke! It *did* like it!

"Yes!" cried Grandad. And he and Zac laughed too. He was talking normally again!

At that very moment, the clock struck five. Just in time! Grandad struggled to his feet and he and Zac did a dance of triumph around the room. The curse was broken!

Finally, Grandad sank into his chair and he rang Louise. "We did it!" he panted. "We broke the curse!"

"Congratulations!" she cried. "I'm coming right round. I need to see this Sapphire Skull for myself!"

★★★

Zac and Grandad were just eating their second helping of triple chocolate-chip ice cream to celebrate when there was a knock at the door. It was Louise. And she was carrying a big, heavy, box.

"What on earth's that?" asked Grandad.

"If I can bring it inside, I'll show you!" panted Louise. "Quick! It's heavy!"

They stepped back and she carefully put the big box on their hall table and opened it up. Grandad and Zac eagerly peered inside as Louise carefully took out an amazing stone tiger! It had fierce red eyes and its mouth was open in a huge roar.

"Wow!" Zac exclaimed.

"This," said Louise, smiling, "is the Terrifying Tiger of Troy. It's a family heirloom. I offered it to the museum but they won't touch it because it's supposed to be cursed too. And, well, you did so well breaking the curse of the

Sapphire Skull, I wondered if you'd like to try this one too? I bet you'll find it's a piece of cake!"

"Yeah! Wicked!" cried Zac, reaching for it.

"Oh no!" said Grandad, laughing. "You're not going anywhere near this one, Zac. Not after last time."

"But Grandad!" Zac protested. "I've learnt my lesson and I'll handle this tiger very, very carefully. And we made a pretty awesome team on the last curse! Ancient Greek artefacts are so cool... could you teach me more about them? Pleeease?!"

Grandad hesitated.

Louise laughed. "Seems like you've got another budding young archaeologist in the family!"

Grandad smiled. "Seems I have," he said. "Okay, Zac, we'll work together on this one too."

"Yes!" cried Zac, triumphantly—making sure not to wave his arms anywhere near the tiger!

Discussion Points

1. Where does Zac find the Sapphire Skull in the beginning?

2. How does Grandad get cursed by the skull?

a) He knocks it to the floor

b) He leaves it at the museum

c) He takes the sapphires

3. What was your favourite part of the story?

4. What language does Grandad have to use to break the curse?

5. Why do you think the skull had to hear a joke to break the curse?

6. Who was your favourite character and why?

7. There were moments in the story when Zac had to **solve difficult problems**. Where do you think the story shows him doing this most successfully?

8. What do you think happens after the end of the story?

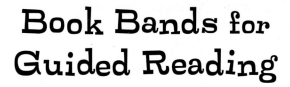

Book Bands for Guided Reading

Pink
Red
Yellow
Blue
Green
Orange
Turquoise
Purple
Gold
White
Lime
Brown
Grey

The Institute of Education book banding system is a scale of colours that reflects the various levels of reading difficulty. The bands are assigned by taking into account the content, the language style, the layout and phonics. Word, phrase and sentence level work is also taken into consideration.

The Maverick Readers Scheme is a bright, attractive range of books covering the pink to grey bands. All of these books have been book banded for guided reading to the industry standard and edited by a leading educational consultant.

To view the whole Maverick Readers scheme, visit our website at
www.maverickearlyreaders.com

Or scan the QR code to view our scheme instantly!

Maverick Chapter Readers
(From Lime to Grey Band)